Ducktails

Janette Oke's Animal Friends

JANETTE OKE'S

Animal Friends

Ducktails

Illustrated by Nancy Munger

BETHANY BACKYARD®

Ducktails
Revised, full-color edition 2001
Copyright © 1985, 2001
Janette Oke

Illustrations by Nancy Munger
Design by Jennifer Parker

Published by Bethany House Publishers
A Ministry of Bethany Fellowship International
11400 Hampshire Avenue South
Minneapolis, Minnesota 55438
www.bethanyhouse.com

Printed in China

Library of Congress Catalog Number 00011556

ISBN 0-7642-2450-6

Dedicated with love to the children
of our Sunday school class at
St. Mark Missionary Church.
May God richly bless you.

JANETTE OKE was born in Champion, Alberta, during the depression years, to a Canadian prairie farmer and his wife. She is a graduate of Mountain View Bible College in Didsbury, Alberta, where she met her husband, Edward. Both Janette and Edward have been active in their local church as Sunday school teachers and board members. The Okes have four grown children and several grandchildren and make their home near Calgary, Alberta.

CHAPTER
One

Today was a very important day for me. Today was the day I hatched out of my egg. It took most of the morning, so once I was finished I took a long nap. When I awoke, there was a lot going on around me.

I struggled to my feet and looked about. My feet worked a little better now. Earlier today they didn't work at all. Now I could even lift my body up a bit so that I could move forward by pushing along on my tummy.

"Isn't it wonderful!" said a voice beside me.

I looked up. It was so far up. It seemed that there was just no top to this world, it was so very far away.

I wasn't alone. We were in the nest. There were a number of us. The others all looked alike. I looked down at myself to see if I looked like them, too. I wasn't sure.

There was only one more egg to go. He was working very hard, pecking at the shell and pushing at it from the inside. Soon he would be free.

All of a sudden, someone very big and very different from us appeared. She had been stand-ing close by. She reached down a long neck and spoke to us.

"Hello, children," she said, and there was love in her voice. "You are all here. That's nice. It's so good to see you. We've been waiting a long time. I am your mother,

and you are my children. That makes us
family."

"Wow!" I exclaimed. "That's so much to
sort out."

She smiled right at me, just as though I
were the only one in the nest. "You'll soon
have it all figured out," she assured me.

She talked to some of the others then,
saying words of greeting and love and nuz-
zling them with her long, orange bill.

The last little one broke free of the shell
just then, and a cry of celebration went up.
We all were free.

Our big-creature mother looked
pleased, too. "You're all here," she said again
happily. "All nine of you. I can hardly wait
for your father to see you."

"Father?" I asked curiously.

"Yes, your father. He's part of the family, too."

"Is he like us?" a little voice beside me asked before I could.

"Oh my, no," said our mother. "He is much bigger than you. He is even bigger than I am."

There were gasps from the nest. We couldn't imagine someone even bigger than our mother.

"You should sleep now," said Mother. "You've all had a very busy day."

She arranged us in the nest and moved over us. She lowered her warm, fluffy body ever so gently to cover us with her soft feathers. The bright sun was blotted out, and we soon began to feel the warmth of her and of one another. I felt very sleepy. I curled my head under my wing again and slept.

CHAPTER
Two

"Wake up, wake up," Mother was saying. "Your father's here. He's anxious to meet you."

I opened my eyes. A big creature, who looked much like Mother, was bending over us. He looked very happy. Carefully he counted each of us. Perhaps he counted all of our wings and feet, too. He studied us, and he seemed pleased with what he found.

"This is your father," Mother said again.

"Hello there," said the big creature. "I'm glad that you have all arrived safely."

Mother began her introductions. "This is Boyd, and Hiram, Prudence, Hazel, Gertrude, and Oscar. And this is Fluff," she said, indicating the tiny, giggling one. "This is Zackery." She nodded her head at the one who stood so very close to me with a twinkle in his eye.

And then she turned to me. "And this is Quackery."

Quackery! So that was me!

I turned to the one named Zackery and smiled.

"Hey," he said, his eyes still twinkling. "Our names rhyme—Zackery and Quackery."

I liked him, this new brother. I had a feeling that we'd get along just fine. But before we had a chance to talk any more, Mother was stirring us up again.

"Come on, now. It's time to be up and on our way. We have much to learn."

The whole nest was stirring—all nine of us.

"First you need to learn how to eat,"

Mother continued.

"Eat?" I had never heard of eating.

"Follow me," urged Mother. She left the nest, and we scrambled to follow her.

It was only one small step for Mother to leave the nest. But it was like crossing a mountain to the rest of us. We struggled up the steep slope, pushing with our feet as well as with our short, stubby wings. It was hard going up and messy work coming down. One by one, we reached the edge of the long climb up, and then went sprawling down on the other side.

We gathered ourselves from the dust, scrambled to our feet, and hurried after Mother.

CHAPTER Three

We reached an area where all kinds of creatures were together. Some walked well, some waddled or tumbled like us, and others just seemed to float along. I looked about curiously. It was kind of scary. Was it safe to go in there?

But Father did not hesitate. He walked right into the midst of the bunch, with Mother following closely behind him. We had been told to follow, so we moved forward also.

We came to a container with something in it.

"This is water," Mother said. "We all need water in order to live."

She put her bill in the water, and then lifted her long neck upward. Her bill stretched in the air. Something along her neck sort of bounced. Father did the same thing.

"Now you try it," he said. "You fill your bill with the water, and then lift your head high and swallow."

We tried. Most of us tumbled forward into the water and flopped about on our tummies in our effort to get out again. It wasn't as easy as it looked. It was wet. We got up, shaking the drops of water from our downy feathers, not sure if we liked the feel of it. We tried again. It seemed that our bills just wouldn't go down without the rest of us following.

It took several tries before I was able to get a little of the water where it belonged— down my throat. Once I had caught on, I liked the feel and the taste of it. I drank more. I was not good at it, but I was learning.

We moved on from the water to an area where the ground was covered with little round things.

"Now you must eat," said Mother.

At first I had no idea what we were to do. Mother and Father tried to show us.

"Like this," said Mother, and she pecked at the ground.

"Like this," I repeated and pecked at the ground, too.

My sister giggled and followed our example.

It was hard for me to understand. What was so special about eating? Then I noticed that Father and Mother weren't just pecking at the ground. When they lifted their beaks, they actually had something in them. Bits of something lay scattered all over the ground, and they were busy picking them up.

I decided to follow their example. I picked one up. It fell before I could even lift it. I tried again. Once more I lost it. I chose a smaller one and tried again. On my fifth try with the smaller one I was able to lift it from the ground.

What do I do with it now? I wondered. I watched Father to see, but when I lifted my head to observe him, I lost it again and had to start all over.

"No, no. Not like that," Mother said softly. "You eat it. Like this."

She reached down, took a bite off the ground, held it securely in her bill, and then, with a quick outward motion of her long neck, the piece disappeared. She had swallowed it! It was amazing.

Finally, I got it to work. I kept going,

picking up more pieces and swallowing them. A strange thing happened. My tummy stopped hurting. I was feeling nice and full and even getting sleepy. I noticed that the others began to look like I was feeling. I heard my father and mother talking.

"Perhaps that is long enough for their first outing," my father was saying.

Mother looked about. "I think you're right," she said. "They look tired. Let's take them home."

We tumbled along behind them and scurried back to our nest. One by one we tumbled into the nest and lay on the softness of the bottom. It was so good to be home. It was good to be able to rest our tired little bodies. It was even good to feel the warmth of Mother's softness, though the day had not been cold.

We snuggled down, put our heads

under our wings, and cuddled up together.
So much had happened in the last few hours
that I couldn't believe how my world had
changed. I could hardly wait for more dis-
coveries. But for now I was too tired to even
think about it. I shut my eyes and let sleep
come.

CHAPTER
Four

"Come," Mother was saying.

"But I'm not hungry yet," I argued sleepily.

She laughed at me. "Well, we do have things to do besides eat," she said. "It's time to go to the pond."

"The pond?"

"You'll see. Come on, sleepyhead."

She stepped off the nest and called to us to follow. It was still a big climb, even though my legs felt much stronger and steadier. We tumbled out one by one, following the lead of our father and mother.

I hurried to keep up with my father. Zackery was panting along at my side, and

Fluff was not far behind us.

"Wait for me," she cried as she tried to catch up.

Father slowed down so that it would be easier for us to stay with him. I could hear Mother still urging on the ones who were falling behind at the end of the line.

At last we reached a very strange-looking thing. It lay out before us, shining in the morning sun. Grass and trees grew all around it.

Father waited until we were all next to him. Then he did a very strange thing. He left the solid ground and walked right out into the thing called the pond. It came up on his legs instead of letting him walk on top of it.

I thought that he would fall right in,
but he stepped forward again and sat right
on the water! He moved out slowly. Then he
turned around and came back toward us.

I stood with my mouth open, watching
him. How did he do that?

"Go on," urged Mother. "Follow your
father."

I wanted to try it. And I would have
jumped right in, but Prudence was standing
in my way.

"It'll go right over my head," she
wailed. "Father's big, but I'll . . . I'll just
sink!"

"No," laughed Mother. "You will swim
just like your father. Now, go on. Try it."

Still Prudence waited. I scrambled
around her and put my foot into the wet-
ness, testing it. *Should I trust it? Will I really
float on top?*

CHAPTER
Five

I took a step and held my breath. It worked! I was still on top of the water, even though my feet could no longer touch ground. It was amazing.

My father circled around beside me. He was smiling at me.

"Good," he said. "Now, give a push—like this, your foot against the water."

I tried and gave a push. To my great surprise, I moved forward. I gave another hard push, and another, and ran smack into a cluster of grass.

I could hear Father laughing softly. He reached out his long bill and pulled me back gently.

"You need to learn to use both feet," he told me. "That way you can learn to steer. If you want to turn this way, you push hard with this foot. If you want to turn that way, you push with the other foot."

I tried it. It really did work. It took me a while to get it working just right, but when I did, it was fun. I loved it.

Zackery was beside me now.

"Look," I called to him. "I'm doing it. Look."

The others all joined us and were swimming around the pond, too. There were calls and cries of excitement. It seemed that all of us felt good about the water.

Fluff was giggling again. "I can do it. Just look at me. I can do it!"

"Now," said Mother when the excitement died down some. "Follow us." She led the way, and the rest of us sped up our

kicking little feet so that we could follow.

At first we swam slowly around the pond—slowly for Mother and Father, that is. The rest of us had to work quite hard at it. Father and Mother checked on us and sometimes offered advice on our stroke or our steering.

Prudence still swam as though she feared that the water might suddenly change its mind and decide to pull her under.

"Loosen up, dear," I heard Mother say to her. "Just relax and let the water hold you. Like this. Come on, relax. Trust it."

Prudence loosened up some, but she did not relax.

We moved on farther, slowly moving in and out of the reeds and water plants.

"Now," said Father. "We taught you how to find food in the farmyard. Today we are going to teach you how to find food in the water."

I looked around me for scattered grain but saw none.

"The water is full of tasty things," Father went on. "You just need to know how to look for them. Watch closely."

And with those words, both Father and Mother began to point out things that were good to eat. The food floated on the surface of the water or under the leaves of the growing things. We soon learned to spot it.

Every now and then, Father or Mother would look about and take count to make sure that all of us were gathered around them. If some of us strayed a bit far, we were called to get back together with the rest of the family.

Once it looked like we were able to find food on the pond, Father decided that it was time for another lesson.

CHAPTER
Six

Father looked each of us in the eyes. "You have learned of all the good things on the pond surface. Now we will show you what else we are able to do." And with those words he gave a quick flip and disappeared completely from our sight. We all gasped. Amazing!

As the minutes ticked by slowly, we all became scared. Prudence even began to cry. She was sure that Father was lost.

I looked at Mother. She did not appear to be worried. But how could he stay under the water for such a long, long time?

At last he came up and smiled at all of us. He had something in his bill. And from the look on his face, I could tell it was tasty.

"Your turn, Mother," he said. And while he watched our anxious faces, Mother disappeared from sight.

She didn't stay as long as Father had. Perhaps she knew that we were still not sure about it all. When she came back up, she had something to eat in her bill. She seemed to enjoy it as she ate it slowly.

"Now it's your turn," said Father.

I couldn't believe that he meant that we would actually be able to do that!

"Watch carefully," he went on. "This is how it is done."

I was excited to get started. The first time that I tried, I just bobbed quickly to the surface again. I tried again, but I kept floating to the top. It seemed that I just couldn't get my little body under the water. But at the third try, I pushed extra hard with my wings, and down I went.

Wow! There were all kinds of things to see under the water.

Zackery was there beside me. All around us were kicking legs and diving bodies.

Each time that I went under, I had to return quickly to the surface for air. I couldn't reach the floor of the pond, where all of the good things seemed to be. I went back up for a good gulp of air and tried once more. I still didn't make it to the bottom. It seemed to be such a very long way away.

Still, it sure was fun to dive. It seemed that all too soon Father was calling us to head back to the farmyard.

CHAPTER
Seven

We swam again in the afternoon. Zackery and I were beginning to feel very strong and fast. We soon began to play games of daring and skill. With Fluff acting as our timekeeper, we would dive and see which one of us could stay under the longest. Sometimes we got so busy playing games that we forgot to eat, and then we felt hungry when we should have been well fed.

After a few days, we were able to reach the bottom of the pond with no trouble at all. We not only fed on the bottom, but we played games on the bottom, as well.

Zackery was usually the one to think them up. But I was always willing to try them. Once, in a game of follow-the-leader, I got caught in some long weeds at the bottom and probably would still be there if quick-thinking Fluff hadn't told Father. With a thrust of his strong bill, he loosened the weeds that bound me. I scurried to the top of the pond for some much needed gulps of air.

Father scolded us and warned us not to take foolish chances underwater, or anywhere for that matter. And for a few days our games were more cautious. But we soon forgot the warning and went back to taking our risks.

We got to be very good swimmers and loved to spend our time in the water. I think that Zackery would have been willing to sleep there if Mother and Father had let him.

We were growing. Oscar was still our

biggest family member and Fluff our smallest, but we were all growing. We never tumbled forward on our faces anymore as we scrambled along, trying to keep pace with Father and Mother. Father did not even have to shorten his stride much anymore.

We spent our days on the pond, with trips to the farmyard for grain, and our nights back in the nest. Our bodies were stronger and our minds more alert. Mother and Father still kept a watchful eye over us, but we were allowed to swim out farther and farther from the rest of the family now. And our curiosity often led us to do just that.

CHAPTER
Eight

Zackery and I began to wonder about the other animals on the pond. Some of them looked like us, but there were some larger, white creatures that did not. They did not talk like us, either, and it took concentration for us to be able to understand them.

We wished to get close enough to ask a few questions, but just as we hoped that we could approach them, Father or Mother would call us.

"Keep with the family, boys," Father ordered, and we had to come back.

Zackery grumbled. "How are we ever going to learn anything if we can't even leave the family?" he complained.

I agreed with him, though I wasn't sure that I should voice it.

"Well, I'm not giving up," Zackery went on. "One of these times Father won't be looking."

Our chance came the next afternoon. I had one eye on Father and the other eye on Zackery as we swam about, getting a little farther from our family and a little closer to the other swimmers on the pond. Suddenly, there was a *swish* sound, and a body surfaced right before our eyes.

It was another of our kind and very close to us. *Why hadn't we thought to do that?* I wondered.

"Hi," said the other fellow.

Zackery moved in closer. "Hi," he answered for us.

"Been watching you," said the other fellow.

"We've been watching you, too," I answered.

"What're your names?" he asked us then.

Zackery took over. "He's Quackery and I'm Zack," he said.

I looked at this brother who had been so excited that our names rhymed. How come he was suddenly Zack? But Zackery paid no attention to my stare.

"My name's Clinton," the other duck went on. "You can call me Clint. Do you live near the pond?"

I thought that it was a silly question. Didn't we all live near the pond?

"Right over there," said Zackery, nodding his head in the direction from which we always came.

"Me too," said Clinton. "Maybe "

But our conversation was interrupted

by Clinton's folks, who called first. We could hear them scolding him as he returned to the circle of his family.

Mother called then, and we got scolded, too.

"Why is it wrong to talk to one of our kind?" I asked her, trying not to sound rude but wanting to know.

"It's not wrong to speak to one of our kind," she informed me. "We often visit with them, but not when we have a family to train and care for. When we are training our family, that comes first and takes all of our time and attention. And as long as you are in training, you stay with the family and learn the rules and the dangers. The others aren't ready to venture out yet—in fact, you and your brother need to learn more caution, as well. This time you only spoke to a duck. But it could have been someone who might have brought you harm. You must wait for our instructions before you make such moves."

I wondered if Zackery had been listening and if he would obey Mother. What she said made sense to me. We didn't know our friends from our enemies. We would do well to listen to Mother and Father and to take each step forward only as they saw us ready for it.

CHAPTER
Nine

We were changing. Among the soft fluff of our downy feathers, stiffer, darker feathers were coming in. We were growing up, and Zackery and I took great pride in the fact.

"Soon we won't need to listen to Mother and Father anymore," said Zackery. "They have too many rules. Anyway, I don't think that there are even any enemies around here. I haven't seen any. Have you?"

"Well . . . no," I stammered. "But if they say—"

Gertrude overheard the conversation and quickly butted in. "You'd better behave or I'll tell Mother," she warned. "You're just asking for trouble. If Father and Mother say that there are enemies, then you can be sure—"

But Zackery cut in, his annoyance showing. "Why don't you just buzz off," he said angrily. "You're always being bossy, telling everybody else how to live."

I was afraid that there was going to be a fight. But before it could really get started, Father appeared and both of them wisely stopped. I knew that the fight would continue when Father was not around. I hoped that I wouldn't be around, either.

"We are going to the farmyard for the evening feeding," Father said. "Everyone ready?"

I quickly fell into line, and Zackery, who was still angry, fell in beside me.

When we got to the yard, there were many others there already feeding. I spotted

Clinton almost immediately, and I guessed that Zackery did, too. I noticed that he was trying to work his way toward Clinton as we fed. Mother and Father were not watching. They were busy searching out and eating the scattered grain.

"Keep moving over toward that corner, and don't forget to call me Zack," Zackery said to me. I was curious, too, about this new creature, and so I allowed myself to be guided slowly, steadily, toward the other side of the circle.

When we got within speaking distance, Zackery spoke softly, "Hi."

Clinton answered back just as quietly, "Hi."

"How ya doing?" said Zackery—Zack.

"Great. How ya doing?"

"Good. Ya have a good swim today?" asked Zack.

"Yeah. We learned how to stay under for a long time."

"Quack and I already know that," boasted Zack.

I looked at him. It was one thing for him to insist upon being called Zack. But it was quite another thing for him to decide to call me Quack. I didn't like it, but I didn't say anything.

"I was talking to one of the older guys," went on Clinton. "He says that we don't know anything about the fun of the pond. He says to just wait until a real good wind comes up. That's when swimming is fun. The waves lift you way up and then drop you way down. Just like a great big roller coaster—up and down."

"Boy, that sounds fun," Zack was saying. "I hope that the wind blows soon. I can hardly wait to try it."

"It's not too good on our pond," Clinton went on. "It's too sheltered. He says that the pond across the road gets much higher waves because it is bigger and more open to the wind."

We were forbidden to cross the road, and according to Father and Mother, so were the offspring of the other families.

"He's tried it?" asked Zack, his eyes big.

"Does it all the time," went on Clinton. "I'm gonna try it, too, the first chance that I get."

Just then there was a loud call. "Mother," yelled Gertrude in her loudest, most offensive voice. "Zackery and Quackery are off talking to strangers again."

I could feel the anger in Zackery. Not only had Gertrude brought us to the attention of our parents, but to every creature in the yard. It made us sound like little kids.

Father's voice quickly spoke to us, "Boys—over here." And we went back to join the family.

Zackery was so cross that his face was red. I didn't feel so great myself, being embarrassed like that right out in front of everyone. But I said nothing.

CHAPTER
Ten

That night, after we had all been bedded down, I couldn't sleep. There were so many things that I didn't know or understand. I decided to have a little talk with Mother. I squeezed out from under her wing and moved up beside her.

She turned and looked at me and rubbed me gently with her beak. I wished that she wouldn't do that. It made me feel like a little child again. I looked around to see if anybody had been watching. There was no one. Well, as long as no one was looking, I guess Mother could do it.

"I can't sleep," I complained.

"Want to talk?" she asked.

Now, how does she know that? I wondered but didn't ask.

"We met a guy today," I said in what I
hoped was an off-hand manner.

"I noticed," said Mother.

"His name's Clinton," I went on.

"We know his family," said Mother.

"Are they—are they a nice family?" I
asked her, hoping that she wouldn't object
to us knowing Clinton.

"A fine family—
though I think that
Clinton might be
just a little stub-
born. They worry
about him."

I thought of Clinton and his determina-
tion to visit the other pond on his own. I
wondered if Mother knew about his plans.
But she didn't say any more.

"Why do you say that?" I asked after waiting for a few minutes.

"I've been watching. His mother and father have trouble keeping him in line, and she has told me that they are concerned."

"It's not wrong to want to learn about things, is it?" My anger showed in my voice in spite of my effort to keep it out.

"Oh no," said Mother hastily. "It's not wrong at all to be curious about life and all that is around us. We just need to be cautious, that's all. We need to learn to accept advice and direction from someone else who has been around longer than we have, and to listen to their judgment on some things. Your father is very wise and has lived for a number of years. When he advises against something, you would be wise to listen."

I didn't say anything for a moment. I hated to argue with Mother, but I did think that she was going a bit too far. It seemed perfectly safe about the farm and the pond. I still hadn't seen anything that looked like an enemy, and neither had Zack. We both had our eyes and ears open. I thought that perhaps both Father and Mother were a bit too cautious with age. Were all old folks like that?

"You're in too big a hurry, Quackery," Mother went on. "You will be given much more freedom as time goes on. Believe me. We'll know when you are ready to be on your own. And now, young man," she said, "You'd better get back to bed. It's getting late, and you should be sleeping. Tomorrow will be another big day."

I wanted to protest and ask more questions, but I knew that Mother expected to be obeyed. I told her good-night and pushed back under her wing.

It was still hard to go to sleep. There were so many things to think about. So many things to learn. It seemed that I was the only one who ever asked questions. Even Zack didn't bother asking. He planned to find the answers for all of his questions on his own. Maybe Zack was right. I didn't know. Maybe one shouldn't bother asking but should just look for the answers. Maybe one should just be free to choose his own friends and take the consequences if he made wrong choices. I didn't see how much harm could come to one by doing that.

"Quackery," Zack said, "there's really good picking over here."

It seemed Zack had something on his mind besides the food on the ground. I followed him.

As soon as we were out of earshot, Zack pulled me aside and whispered, "Remember what Clinton said about the big pond?"

"You mean the one across the road?"

"Right. Well, some of the chickens are saying that there is to be a real big wind today. Clinton says that it would be a great day to try the pond. How about it?"

"I don't know," I hesitated. "I'm not sure that Mother would—"

But Zackery cut me short. "Mother doesn't need to know. She is busy visiting now, and we could sneak off without her even seeing us."

"Father might—" I began, but Zack stopped me on that, too.

"Father's way over there," he said, nodding his head at the far corner of the yard, where Father was feeding and chatting with some of the other ducks.

"I don't think we should," I said quietly.

"Then you don't want to come?"

"Well, I want to, but I don't think that we should."

"Okay, you big sissy. Stay here if you want to. Miss all the fun. I don't care. I'm going with Clinton."

I cast my eyes around, hoping that Gertrude might be somewhere nearby to tattle on us again. She wasn't. I knew that Zack shouldn't go, but I wasn't about to tell on him and make him mad at me.

"You coming?" asked Clinton.

Zack looked at me. I did not move.

"Well, I am," he answered Clinton. "But I don't think Quack is."

"What's wrong?" asked Clinton. "You a mama's boy?"

He said it in a sing-songy way, and they both laughed at me and moved off.

I could hear them laughing as they went, and I knew that they were laughing at me. "Mama's boy," they had called me. I didn't want to be a mama's boy. At least, I sure didn't want the other fellows thinking of me in that way. But what else could I do?

CHAPTER Twelve

I moved slowly toward my father. He was doing more chatting than eating. He was talking to Mr. Whitehall, the big gander, and to Mr. Lucky of another duck family.

"When did they see him?" I heard Father ask.

"Yesterday," was the answer. "He was in very close to the barn."

"I guess we all need to be extra careful," said Father. "He will be back again for sure."

Even as Father spoke, I saw him look about the farmyard and begin to look for his family. Mother was there. Father's eyes went to her first, and then he began to look for each of the children.

Hiram and Hazel were over near the fence. Gertrude and Fluff were chatting. Prudence, who was always shy and hesitant, stayed close to Mother. And Oscar, who was always boastful because of his size, was busy strutting around for the benefit of the youth of the farmyard.

Father kept on looking. I knew that he was about to ask me the dreaded question. I tried to move away, but I wasn't fast enough.

"Where's Zackery?" he asked me.

I was caught. I looked up, and my eyes traveled around the yard as though I, too, were looking. I didn't know how to answer Father. Zack would never forgive me if I told on him, yet how could I tell a lie?

"Zack?" I said lamely, in an effort to conceal what I knew.

"Mr. Whitehall says that a hawk has

been seen hanging around."

"Is . . . is . . . a hawk dangerous?" I stammered. I had never met a hawk before.

"Extremely dangerous," said Father. "Especially to the young. He can snatch a youngster before they even know what his shadow means."

I felt nervous then. What if something happened to Zack? I was about to tell all I knew to Father, but before I could say anything, he moved abruptly away. He went to talk with Mother, concern showing in his face.

They soon gathered all of us together and headed us to the pond. It was clear that they felt safer where they would have the protection of a dive if the hawk should appear again. I could tell that they were worried about Zack. I was worried, too. I did wish that he would hurry back.

The wind did begin to blow. It made waves on the pond. At first, they were gentle. I loved the feeling of being lifted slightly and then swished down. As the afternoon went on, the wind became stronger and stronger. I still loved the feeling. It was like a thrill ride. Up and down, up and down, we rode the waves.

I knew that Mother and Father were both still worried about Zack. I heard them ask the other family members if they had seen Zackery leave the yard. They all said that they hadn't. Gertrude had to add her piece about Zackery hanging out with the wrong crowd and asking for trouble. Mother made no comment, but the troubled look in her eyes increased.

It was mid-afternoon before I noticed Zack swimming toward us. He dove for the last distance and came to the surface again

right in the midst of the family. I knew he hoped that Father and Mother hadn't even noticed that he had been missing and that he could just sneak back in. It didn't work. As soon as he surfaced, Father was beside him.

"Where have you been?" Father asked.

Zackery gave me a you'd-better-not-tell look. Then he looked back at Father.

I knew that Zackery wanted to say that he had been right there all of the time. I also knew that he could tell by Father's face that it would be silly to say that. Father knew that he had not been there.

"I got separated, I guess," said Zack. "I didn't see you leave the farmyard. I went back to the nest, but you weren't there. So I came over here."

Father looked doubtful. I didn't think that he really believed Zack, but he didn't say that he didn't. Instead he said, "Well, you were separated for an awfully long time. I would suggest that in the future, you pay more attention to what you are doing—and to what the rest of the family is doing. There is a hawk hanging around. It's extremely dangerous, and I want you to have the protection of the family and the pond. You stay with the family from now on."

"Yes, sir," said Zack reluctantly, and yet with relief.

It had worked. He had gotten away with it. It made me wonder if he'd be smart enough to leave well enough alone, or if he'd try it again.

CHAPTER Thirteen

"You should have been with us," Zack whispered to me later that night when we were tucked under Mother's wings and were supposed to be sleeping. "I've never had so much fun in my life."

"We had waves here, too," I said stubbornly.

"Nothing like we had. Boy, was it fun. I can hardly wait for another wind."

"You're not going again, are you?" I asked, shocked. "You heard what Father said."

"A hawk," said Zack. "He'd keep me here, missing out on all the fun, just because of a hawk."

"Hawks are dangerous. They like baby ducks."

"Well, I'm not a baby duck," declared Zack hotly. "Haven't you noticed? I'm not a kid anymore, Quack. I want to have some fun in life. I'm not going to sit around here tied to the folds just—"

"You're taking chances, can't you see that?" I argued.

"Oh, phooey," said Zack. "You sit around and be Mama's good little boy if you want to. Me, I'm going to have some fun out of life."

I wanted to have fun, too. Yet I wasn't about to disobey the advice and orders of my parents in order to do it.

The next day it was calm on the pond when we first entered the water. I kept thinking of the fun waves the day before and hoped that the wind would blow again.

I also thought of Zack and his fun on the open pond. It must have been a great deal more fun to rock up and down on the higher waves. Would it hurt if I went just once?

CHAPTER
Fourteen

L ater that week, we went to the pond as soon as we had finished breakfast. It was a calm morning and the feeding was good. I was having a lot of fun eating and diving. I loved the water. I loved the feeling of strength in my feet as I pushed myself forward and then down, down, down.

I'm getting to be a pretty strong swimmer, I thought, very proud of myself.

I was swimming along quietly when there was a sharp cry from my Mother. There were splashes all around me. I took a moment to look instead of doing as Father and Mother had drilled us. We had been taught to dive immediately when the alarm sounded, without a second to lose. The brief look up was a big mistake, for there, above my head and swooping down at an alarming rate of speed, was the hawk.

He looked so fast, so powerful, so frightening, and I ducked under the water just as I heard the splash of his wings hitting the water above me. He pulled out of his dive and climbed back into the sky.

My heart was pounding. My head spinning. I stayed underwater for as long as I could, not knowing if I dared to ever surface again. At last my lungs could stand it no longer, and I arose from the water's depths, looking nervously about.

Father, Mother, and the family were swimming some distance from me. With panic still clutching at me, I swam to join them.

Just as I drew near to the family, there

was a cry of "Dive!" from Father, and a shadow passed over my head. I knew without looking up that it was the hawk again, and I did not wait for a second signal. Again I heard the swish above me.

This time as I swam under, I made an effort to stay near the family. We stayed under for as long as we could and then surfaced again. Father kept a sharp eye out and soon commanded us to dive again. It was a terrible feeling, knowing that the hawk circled in the sky above us, ready to drop down the moment that we came back up.

We swam, then dived, resurfaced, and swam, then dived again. I noticed that each time that we resurfaced we were closer to the reeds that grew along one side of the pond. Father was carefully steering us in that direction.

At last we reached the reeds. I felt a little safer, though Father and Mother kept an eye on the sky.

It was several moments before my heart was beating at a normal rate. I knew that the others were just as frightened as I. We all knew that had we been on the ground instead of in the water, things would have been much different. In the water, we were mobile and could dive and hide for many minutes at a time. On land, we were slow and somewhat awkward. Unless we had found something to hide under very quickly, one or two of us most surely would have been missing.

I was thankful for the wisdom of our father and mother. They knew how to protect us.

CHAPTER
Fifteen

Later that night, after we had all been asleep for several hours, I heard whispering. I was still half asleep, but I could tell it was Zack's voice. Whom was he talking to?

I waited until he had come back to the nest, and then I nudged him with my wing.

"What were you doing up? It's the middle of the night," I asked him.

Zack looked down at his feet. I could tell he was embarrassed.

"I was talking with Father. I told him that I'd gone across the road to the big pond," Zack said.

"You what?" I was shocked. Why had

Zack confessed?

Zack seemed to understand what I was thinking. He settled down next to me and began to talk.

"Well, after what happened today with the hawk, I got really scared. I realized that Mother and Father do know a lot more than I do. And even though I may not always like their rules, I need to listen to them and do what they tell me. I was wrong to think I could make it in this world without their rules."

I smiled at Zack. I was relieved, too. "Does this mean you won't be going over to the big pond anymore?" I asked him.

"No way. Actually, I was scared the whole time I was there. It wasn't any fun. I told Father that he could count on me to obey the rules."

"That's great, Zack," I said. "From now

on, we'll stick together."

"Yeah, Quackery. Let's stick together."
Zack smiled at me.

I smiled back. I was very happy to have
my brother back. We snuggled under
Mother's wing and went to sleep.